P9-BZU-588

A Gift for Nana

For my nieces,
Sarah and Amy

Copyright © 2022 by Lane Smith
All rights reserved. Published in the United States by Random House Studio,
an imprint of Random House Children's Books, a division of Penguin Random House LLC, New York.
Random House Studio and the colophon are registered trademarks of Penguin Random House LLC.
Visit us on the Web! rhcbooks.com
Educators and librarians, for a variety of teaching tools, visit us at RHTeachersLibrarians.com
Library of Congress Cataloging-in-Publication Data
Names: Smith, Lane, author.
Title: A gift for Nana / by Lane Smith.
Description: First edition. | New York : Random House Studio, [2022] | Audience: Ages 3–7. |
Summary: "A little rabbit is on the hunt for the perfect gift for his grandmother" —Provided by publisher.
Identifiers: LCCN 2021009691 | ISBN 978-0-593-43033-0 (trade) | ISBN 978-0-593-43034-7 (lib. bdg.) |
ISBN 978-0-593-43035-4 (ebook)
Subjects: CYAC: Rabbits—Fiction. | Gifts—Fiction. | Grandmothers—Fiction. | LCGFT: Picture books.
Classification: LCC PZ7.S6538 Gi 2022 | DDC [E]—dc23
The text of this book is set in Garamond Premier Pro Regular and the display is set in Requiem Fine from the
Hoefler Type Foundry.
The illustrations for this book are mixed media. They were painted in gesso, oils, and cold wax and drawn with an
Apple Pencil in Procreate.
ISBN 978-0-593-70275-8 (proprietary)
MANUFACTURED IN CHINA   10 9 8 7 6 5 4 3 2 1

This Imagination Library edition is published by Random House Children's Books, a division of Penguin Random House LLC, exclusively for
Dolly Parton's Imagination Library, a not-for-profit program dedicated to inspire a love of reading and learning, sponsored in part by
The Dollywood Foundation. Penguin Random House's trade editions of this work are available where all books are sold.

A Gift for Nana

Lane Smith

design by Molly Leach

RANDOM HOUSE STUDIO · NEW YORK

It was not his Nana's birthday.

It was not even a major hare holiday.

But Rabbit wanted to give his Nana a gift anyway.

A crow told him of
a *perfect gift* and
said it was not far.

This sounded
to Rabbit like
a worthy quest.

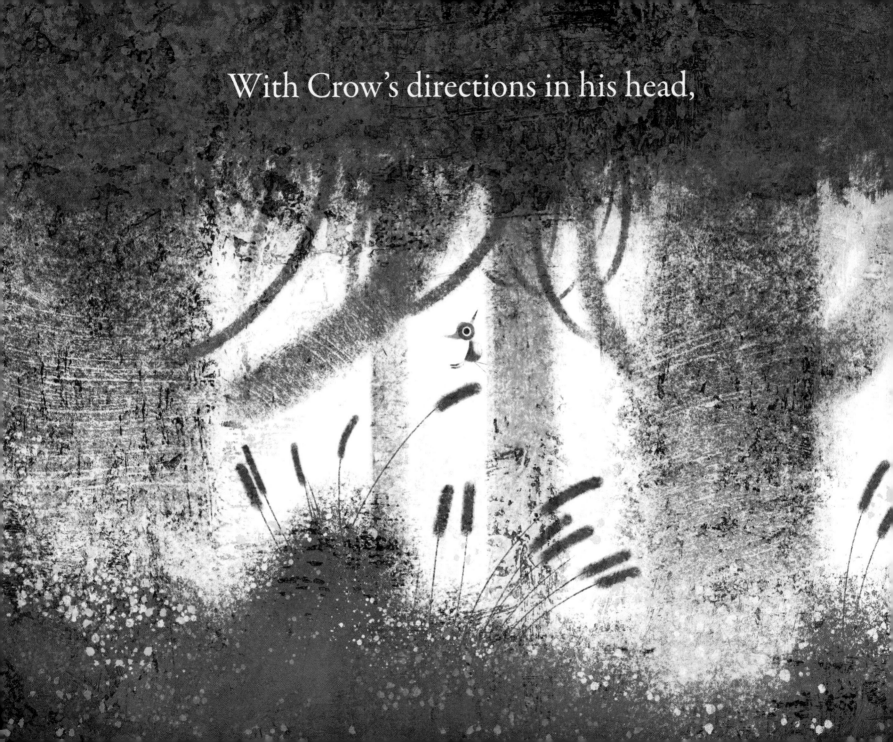

With Crow's directions in his head,

Rabbit began his journey through a green and grand forest.

He had not gone far when he met a full moon.

"Hello," said Rabbit. "Shouldn't you be in the sky?"

"Not for a few more hours," said the moon.
"You can always find me down here while the sun is up there."

Rabbit told the moon of his quest for Nana's *perfect gift*.

"Does your Nana need a smile?" said the moon.

"I can give her one of my phases."

The moon showed him,
becoming a crescent smile.

"No, my Nana already has a smile as bright as the sun."

At this, the moon grew quiet.

And Rabbit wondered if comparing his Nana's smile
to the sun was not something to say to a moon.

Farther into the woods,
where it was hard to tell
the shadows from the
trees, the forest creatures
became less ordinary.

One was a stickler.

Rabbit told it of his quest
for Nana's *perfect gift*.

"Does your Nana need a **stick**?" asked the stickler.

"She already has a very nice walking stick," said Rabbit. "But between you and me, I don't think she really needs it."

Next Rabbit crossed a **big big** lake.

A **big big** fish asked him where he was going.

Rabbit told of his quest for Nana's *perfect gift.*

"Would your Nana like some water?" said the big big fish.
"I have saved some in a cup. It is around here somewhere.
I'm sure I can find it."

"No, thank you. My Nana already
has a glass of water next to the chair
where she reads to me," said Rabbit.

Rabbit landed on a rocky shore.

"Ahoy, Mountain," he said.

"I am not a mountain. I am a volcano!" boomed a volcano.

"Apologies," said Rabbit.
And once again, he told of his quest for Nana's *perfect gift*.

"Does your Nana have a temper?"

"I'm not sure what that is," said Rabbit.

The volcano exploded into ten million fireworks.

"Oh yes.
She already
has one of
those.

But I don't see it much."

Now Rabbit stood before a peak dotted with dusty caves.

The peak was steep.

The caves were spooky.

Nana would probably say a comforting something or other about now,
Rabbit thought as his nose began to twitch.

"Ah-choo!" Rabbit sneezed into a dusty cave.
"Ah-choo!" the cave echoed back.

"Bless you," said Rabbit.
"Bless you," echoed the cave.

That is **exactly** what my Nana would say before I climbed
a steep peak dotted with spooky caves, thought Rabbit.

It was the final leg of Rabbit's journey.

As he climbed, he wondered if Crow should have said the *perfect gift* was not far *as the crow flies.*

Because *as the rabbit walks,* it was very far.

At long last, Rabbit was at the end of his quest.

Crow was right.
It was the *perfect gift.*

Rabbit carried it back the way he came,
past the volcano,

past the big big fish,
past the stickler,

past the moon.

And all of them agreed it was the *perfect gift*.

The distance this time seemed much shorter to Rabbit,
who was eager to return to his Nana.

He stopped only once.

For a bite to eat.

And before long, he was at Nana's house.

Nana lived in an old tree with a fence made of carrots beside a carrot field lined with tidy rows of carrots.

"*Nana,* I have brought you a *gift,*" said Rabbit.

"Although, now that I think about it,
perhaps you already have enough carrots."

"But I do not have *this* carrot," said Nana, smiling the sunny smile Rabbit had mentioned to the moon.

"This is a *perfect gift.*

Do you know why?"

Rabbit was pretty sure Nana was going to say *because it came from him.*

She did. His Nana always said the best things.

"Nana," said Rabbit.
    "Have you ever met a stickler?"

"No," said Nana. "Tell me."